Brad

Sarah

Zach

Mary

Geranium Lady

Joy

Michael

Wumphee

COLLECT ALL FOUR BOOKS IN
The Geranium Lady Series

The Upside-Down Frown and Splashes of Joy
A Book About Joy

Super-Scrumptious Jelly Donuts Sprinkled with Hugs
A Book About Hugs

The Pepperoni Parade and the Power of Prayer
A Book About Prayer

The Tasty Taffy Tale and Super-Stretching the Truth
A Book About Honesty

The Geranium Lady Series

The Tasty Taffy Tale and Super-Stretching the Truth

A Book About Honesty

Barbara Johnson

Illustrations by Victoria Ponikvar Frazier

Thomas Nelson, Inc.

Nashville

Barbara Johnson's
The Geranium Lady Series
The Tasty Taffy Tale and Super-Stretching the Truth

Text copyright © 1999 by Barbara Johnson
Illustrations copyright © 1999 by Tommy Nelson™,
a division of Thomas Nelson, Inc.

Concept and Story by A. Clayton

Published in Nashville, Tennessee, by Tommy Nelson™,
a division of Thomas Nelson, Inc. Vice President of Children's Books: Laura Minchew;
Editor: Tama Fortner; Art Director: Karen Phillips.

Scripture quoted from the *International Children's Bible, New Century Version*,
copyright © 1986, 1988 by Word Publishing. Used by permission.

Library of Congress Cataloging-in-Publication Data

Johnson, Barbara (Barbara E.)
     The tasty taffy tale and super-stretching the truth : a book about honesty /
Barbara Johnson ; illustrations by Victoria Ponikvar Frazier.
          p.   cm.—(The Geranium Lady series)
     Summary: When Michael stretches the truth about how he won the taffy-making
contest, the Geranium Lady helps him understand that saying things that are not
true is like mixing bad ingredients into a recipe.
     ISBN 0-8499-5951-9
     [1. Honesty—Fiction. 2. Contests—Fiction. 3. Candy—Fiction. 4. Christian
life—Fiction.] I. Frazier, Victoria Ponikvar, 1966– ill. II. Title. III. Series: Johnson,
Barbara (Barbara E.). Geranium Lady series.
PZ7.J63043Tas   1999
[E]—dc21
                                                                        98-51076
                                                                              CIP
                                                                              AC

Printed in the United States of America
99 00 01 02 03 QPH 9 8 7 6 5 4 3 2 1

LETTER TO PARENTS

Most kids don't set out to be dishonest. They just find themselves in a situation where s-t-r-e-t-c-h-i-n-g the truth a little seems like an easy way out. But the truth can't be stretched any which way we want. Remember, "what" happens to us isn't nearly as important as "how" we handle what happens to us. That is when the whole world is watching to see whether we have character or we are characters!

But how do we explain a concept like truth to children and grandchildren? Well . . . that's where the idea for this fun children's series first popped up. You see, I believe that laughter is the sweetest music that ever greeted the human ear. Throughout these pages, my hope is that kids will laugh—and learn some valuable lessons—as they follow the Geranium Lady on her zany adventures.

We often find ourselves knee-deep in a sticky situation before we realize what has happened. Thankfully, we serve a God who is ready to take our troubles and change them into sparkling treasures. All we have to do is trust Him. Honest!

Joyfully speaking His truth,

The Geranium Lady

The Geranium Lady

"Blend it. Bend it. Shake it. Make it," the Geranium Lady hummed as she mixed the secret ingredients together in a giant bowl.

"Now, it's time to cook it," Michael said, looking at his stopwatch. This was their last secret step. Michael and the Geranium Lady were hoping that this recipe would win next week's "Top Tasting Taffy" contest.

Together, they made the perfect team. The Geranium Lady came up with the secret ingredients, while Michael carefully calculated how long and at what temperature to cook the taffy.

Ding! The timer signaled that the taffy was ready. The Geranium Lady poured the batch of taffy out onto a giant platter. When the taffy was cool, Michael pulled and rolled it into long strips.

"Super-incredulous!" said Michael as he tasted the chewy, gooey taffy.

"Yes," the Geranium Lady said with a smile. "I think this taffy just might win us the First Place trophy!"

On the day of the contest, the judges tasted taffy from everyone who entered. There was thick taffy. Thin taffy. Double-decker taffy. Even really silly taffy.

At last Tommy Teflon, the announcer in the fresh-pressed suit, took the stage to reveal the number of the prize-winning taffy. As the crowd held its breath, Tommy Teflon called out, "Number 12!"

Michael and the Geranium Lady had created the tastiest taffy in town!

As the Geranium Lady and her young friends said a prayer of thanks, Michael sprinted toward the stage. He couldn't believe *he* had won!

After their prayer, the Geranium Lady and the kids looked around
for Michael. But he was already accepting the award . . . *by himself!*

"Congratulations," Tommy Teflon said to Michael. A gleam flashed from the announcer's perfect teeth as he handed Michael the "Top Tasting Taffy" trophy.

"You must really be a great cook to have created this terrific taffy," said Tommy Teflon.

"Yes," Michael bragged. "I just came up with this recipe last week."

Michael's friends could not believe their ears! How could Michael stretch the truth so much? They all knew that the Geranium Lady had put together the secret ingredients for the taffy.

Just then, Michael saw the Geranium Lady in the crowd. He knew he wasn't telling the whole truth, and he began to feel guilty for taking all the credit.

Michael was trying to sneak off the stage when a chef's hat was plopped on his head.

"As a special treat for our audience," said Tommy Teflon, "the winner will now make his tasty taffy right here onstage."

What could Michael do? He knew the exact temperature to cook the taffy and the best way to pull it, but only the Geranium Lady knew the secret ingredients.

Everyone was watching. In order to hide his first lie, Michael decided to try to make the taffy himself.

Michael mixed ketchup, syrup, whipped cream, peanut butter, and pickles with some other items he found on the table. As the ingredients cooked, a neon glow began to sparkle through the mixture.

"Oh my!" exclaimed the Geranium Lady. "That's not my secret recipe." She tried to help Michael, but the judges would not let anyone else on the stage.

When the glowy glob was cool, Michael tried to pick it up. But it slipped out of his hands and bounced across the stage! Wumphee thought it was a ball and dived after it.

Wumphee caught the taffy in midair and started to run. Michael held tight to one end and watched helplessly as the strange taffy stretched and stretched across the stage.

Wumphee circled around and around the stage until Tommy Teflon, the judges, and Michael were completely tangled and twisted in the glowing taffy.

"This tastes terrible," a judge said as he licked the taffy wrapped around his head. "You couldn't have made the winning recipe! You'll have to give back the trophy."

Once untangled, Michael ran straight to the Geranium Lady. Still covered in bits of taffy, he said, "I'm sorry I lied about the recipe. I know God wants me to be honest—even when it's not easy."

"Stretching the truth is always messy," said the Geranium Lady, "just like that stretchy taffy you cooked up today."

Then with a smile, the Geranium Lady added, "When you say things that aren't true—or leave out things that are true—it's like mixing bad ingredients into a recipe. It leaves a bad taste with everyone around you."

Michael agreed, and he promised never to stretch the truth again!

TELL EACH OTHER THE TRUTH.

Zechariah 8:16

MAKE YOUR OWN OLD-FASHIONED TASTY TAFFY WITH THIS SUPER-STRETCHY RECIPE!

The real Geranium Lady, Barbara Johnson, has a special treat for you—a recipe for making your very own tasty taffy! You will need help from Mom or Dad for this recipe.

Cooking Utensils:
heavy saucepan (2-quart)
baking pan (15" x 10" x 1")
candy thermometer
scissors
plastic wrap

Ingredients:
2 cups sugar
¼ teaspoon salt
1 cup water
1 cup light corn syrup
2 tablespoons butter
½ teaspoon peppermint extract (optional)
a few drops of your favorite food coloring

Instructions:
1. Butter the bottom and sides of the saucepan and baking pan.
2. Pour the sugar, salt, water, and corn syrup into the saucepan.

*IMPORTANT: A grownup must do steps 3–6.

3. Cook the mixture over medium-high heat. Stir until it begins to boil. Then reduce the heat to medium-low.
4. Without stirring, continue boiling until the thermometer reads 248° (the firm-ball stage). This will take about 30 to 40 minutes. (If using the cold water method of testing, check after 25 minutes.) Remove the thermometer, and take the saucepan off the burner.
5. Stir in the butter, peppermint extract, and food coloring.
6. Pour the mixture into the buttered baking pan, and let it cool for 15 to 20 minutes. (Be sure that a grownup tests this first.)

7. When the taffy is cool enough to handle, butter your hands. Twist and stretch the taffy until it becomes stiff, about 10 to 15 minutes.

8. Divide the taffy into four equal pieces. Twist and stretch the taffy into long strands that are ½ inch thick. Snip each strand into bite-size pieces using buttered scissors.

9. Wrap each piece of tasty taffy in plastic wrap. Makes about 100 pieces.

Tips for Parents:

This activity offers a perfect chance for you to talk about telling the truth. As you make the taffy, share with your child how stretching the truth is like stretching taffy—it can get really sticky! And the more you stretch the truth, the harder it is to put it all back together again.

Include the entire family by putting a piece of taffy next to each person's plate at dinner. Have everyone tell about a time that he or she stretched the truth—and what happened. Then, as a family, say a prayer asking God for the courage to tell the truth always.